Penguin  Readers

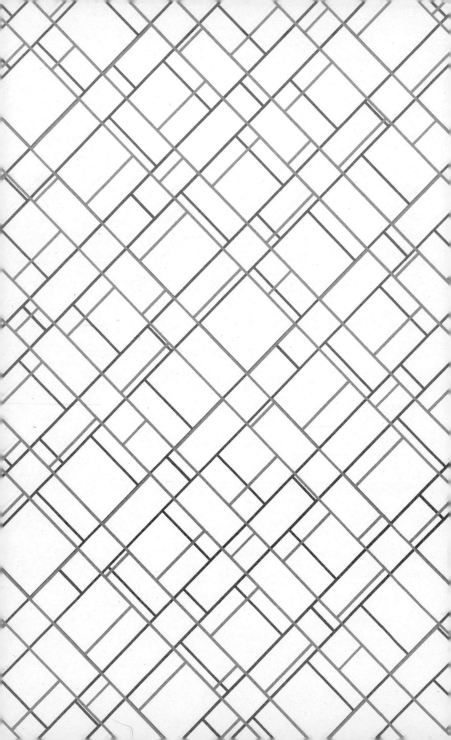

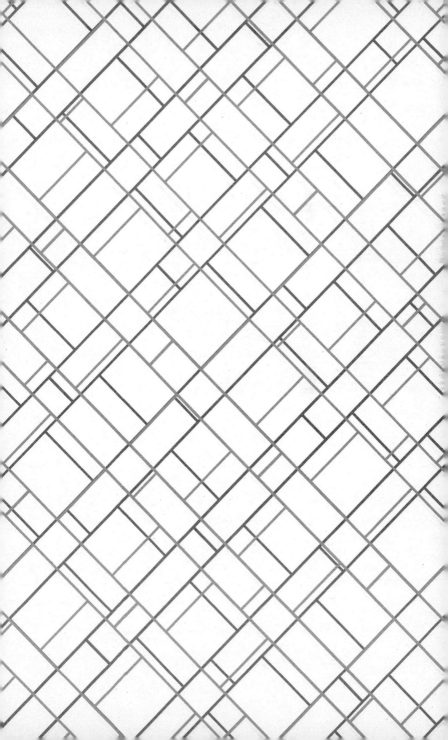

PENGUIN BOOKS

UK | USA | Canada | Ireland | Australia
India | New Zealand | South Africa

Penguin Books is part of the Penguin Random House group of companies
whose addresses can be found at global.penguinrandomhouse.com.
www.penguin.co.uk www.puffin.co.uk www.ladybird.co.uk

Penguin
Random House
UK

First published 2021
001

Text written by Fiona Mackenzie
Text copyright © Penguin Books Ltd, 2021
Illustrated by Dynamo Ltd.
Illustrations copyright © Penguin Books Ltd, 2021
Cover image copyright © Penguin Books Ltd, 2021

Printed and bound in Great Britain by Clays Ltd, Elcograf S.p.A.

The authorized representative in the EEA is Penguin Random House Ireland, Morrison Chambers,
32 Nassau Street, Dublin D02 YH68.

A CIP catalogue record for this book is available from the British Library

ISBN: 978–0–241–49323–6

All correspondence to:
Penguin Books
Penguin Random House Children's
One Embassy Gardens, 8 Viaduct Gardens,
London SW11 7BW

Penguin **Readers**

THE MOOR STONES

FIONA MACKENZIE

LEVEL

ILLUSTRATED BY DYNAMO LTD

SERIES EDITOR: SORREL PITTS

Contents

People in the story

Sheila

Jack

Beth

Mia

Betty

Ralph

Betty's father

Betty's mother

New words

bye

farm

foggy

moors

rainy

Rescue Team

ruin

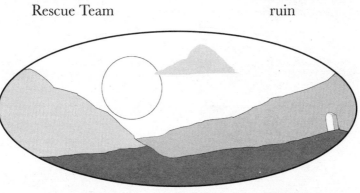

sunny

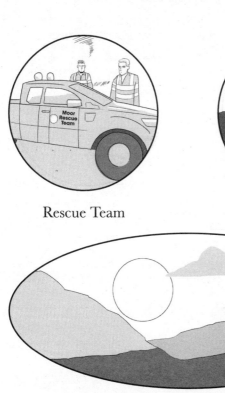

stone

traveller

Before-reading questions

1 Look at the "People in the story" on pages 8–9. Write about these people in your notebook.

   a Sheila

   Sheila has got brown hair. She is wearing a jumper.

   b Beth

   c Mia

   d Betty

   e Ralph

2 Look at the pictures and write the correct word in your notebook.

moors	ruin	farm	stone

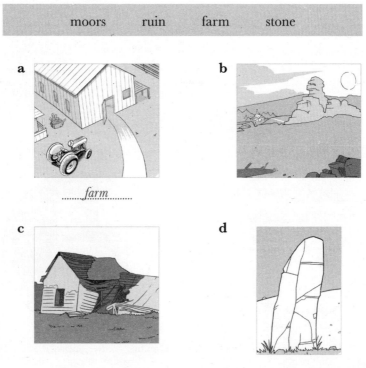

a *farm*

b

c

d

3 Look at the "New words" on pages 10–11 and complete the sentences in your notebook.

  a Sheila says ...._"Bye."_........... to Jack.

  b I'm standing near my friend but I can't see her. It's very ....

  c I'm not going out today. It's foggy and ....

  d It's hot and .... today.

  e My sister helps people on the moors. She works with the ....

  f "The North York Moors are beautiful and lots of .... come here," says Sheila.

4 Look at the pictures and answer the questions.

  a What can you see? Write three sentences about picture A and three sentences about picture B in your notebook.

  b Who are the people, do you think?

A

B

Picture definitions of words in **bold** can be found on pages 10–11

13

THE Moor Stones

It is morning.
Sheila is going to Whitby Station.

Baysdale **Farm**
Bed and Breakfast

Bye!

Are they the **travellers** from New Zealand?

TRAINS

Mia
and
Beth

16

23

Chapter 5: The Moor Stones

Betty lives with her parents, and she works a lot.

She gets milk from the cow.

She cleans. She cooks.

Betty walks on the moors.

Chapter 5: The Moor Stones

She loves the moors.

One day ...

Chapter 5: The Moor Stones

Betty and Ralph meet again. They talk.

They walk on the moors every day.

Chapter 5: The Moor Stones

But Betty meets Ralph every day.

Chapter 5: The Moor Stones

Her parents are angry. It's rainy and cold.

Chapter 5: The Moor Stones

It's **foggy**! Where am I?

Ralph is on the moors, too. He is walking from Midnight Farm.

Where am I?

Chapter 5: The Moor Stones

Chapter 5: The Moor Stones

Chapter 5: The Moor Stones

We can think about Betty and Ralph every day. We can put stones for them on the moors.

Yes.

Chapter 5: The Moor Stones

Travellers sit near Betty's Stone.

1880s

Now

People put money for travellers on Ralph's Stone.

1910s

1930s

The End

Oh, look at my phone!

42

Come in!

Beth is home.

Beth tells her story.

Where does the young man come from?

He lives at Midnight Farm.

During-reading questions

1 Where is Sheila going?
2 Who does Sheila meet? Where do they come from?
3 Does Beth like the North York Moors? Why/Why not?

1 What do people put on the stone?
2 Who is Jack?
3 Do Beth and Mia go to Whitby in the morning? Why/Why not?
4 What does Mia read?

1 What does Betty do on her parents' farm?
2 Who does Betty meet on the moors?
3 Do Betty's parents like her new friend? Why/Why not, do you think?
4 What do travellers do near Betty's Stone? What do people put on Ralph's Stone?

1 Where does Beth go?
2 Who does Jack phone?
3 Who helps Beth?
4 What does Beth tell Sheila, Jack and Mia about him?

After-reading questions

1 After the story, what do Sheila, Jack, Beth and Mia do in the morning? Why?

2 There are three stories in this book. Which people are in the stories?
Story 1: Beth and Mia's story (pages 15–23, 39–45, 50–51)
Story 2: Betty's story (pages 24–38)
Story 3: Beth's story (pages 46–49)

3 Which people do you like and why?

4 Do you like the story? Why/Why not?

5 Would you like to go to the North York Moors? Why/Why not?

Exercises

1 Write the correct verb in your notebook.

1 Sheila **go** / *is going* to Whitby Station.

2 Mia and Beth **is** / **are** travellers from New Zealand.

3 "That **is** / **are** a nice photo."

4 People **puts** / **put** money on the stone.

5 "**Sit** / **sits** here, girls."

6 "You can **come** / **comes** to Whitby with us."

7 "Here **is** / **are** some chocolate for you."

8 Betty **live** /**lives** with her parents.

2 Complete these sentences in your notebook, using the words from the box.

moors	angry	milk	farm
cleans	like	today	cooks

1 Betty gets ....*milk*.......... from the cow.

2 She .... the kitchen.

3 She .... the food.

4 Ralph works on a ....

5 Betty's parents do not .... Ralph.

6 Betty's parents are .... with her.

7 "You can't go on the moors ...."

8 Betty and Ralph meet on the .... every day.

3 Match the two parts of the sentences in your notebook.

Example: 1 – b

1	Come to	**a**	her story.
2	I'm walking	**b**	Baysdale Farm.
3	Look	**c**	cold again.
4	It's rainy and	**d**	find her.
5	We can	**e**	on the moors this morning.
6	Beth tells	**f**	at my phone.
7	Midnight Farm	**g**	Ralph's Stone tomorrow.
8	We can go to	**h**	is a ruin.

4 Complete these sentences in your notebook, using the names from the box.

> Midnight Farm   Sheila and Jack   The Rescue Team
> Ralph's Stone   Mia   Baysdale Farm
> Beth   Betty's Stone

1 *Baysdale Farm* is Sheila and Jack's farm.

2 People put money on ....

3 .... go to Whitby.

4 .... looks at her phone a lot.

5 People sit near ....

6 .... finds Beth's phone.

7 .... goes to Baysdale Farm.

8 .... is a ruin.

5 Complete these sentences in your notebook, using *a*, *the* or *Ø* (no article).

1 It's ....*a*........ beautiful day.
2 Can you take me to ....*Ø*........ Baysdale Farm?
3 Beth is on .... moors.
4 Is that .... Rescue Team?
5 Where does .... young man come from?
6 Midnight Farm is .... ruin.
7 We can go to .... Ralph's Stone tomorrow.
8 We can put .... money there.

6 Complete these sentences in your notebook, using *There is* or *There are*.

1 ......*There are*...... two farms in *The Moor Stones*.
2 .... a cow in Betty's house.
3 .... a clock in Sheila and Jack's kitchen.
4 .... sheep on the moors.
5 .... lots of stories in Sheila's book.
6 .... some chocolate on the table.
7 Write a sentence about the story, using *There is* ....
8 Write a sentence about the story, using *There are* ....

7 Correct these sentences in your notebook.

1 Beth and Mia come from England.
Beth and Mia come from New Zealand.

2 Sheila and Jack meet Beth and Mia at the station.

3 Beth reads a book.

4 Betty meets Ralph at Midnight Farm.

5 Ralph works at Baysdale Farm.

6 The Rescue Team finds Beth on the moors.

8 In your notebook, put these words in the correct group.

live   photo   foggy   angry   work   rainy   beautiful
help   stone   farm   walk   put   traveller   cold   moor

nouns	verbs	adjectives
traveller	*help*	*beautiful*

9 **Put these sentences in the correct order in your notebook.**

a ....Jack phones the Rescue Team again.

b ....Beth tells her story about Ralph.

c ...*1*.....Sheila meets Beth and Mia at Whitby Station.

d ....Beth goes on the moors.

e ....Mia and Beth have dinner with Sheila and Jack.

f ....Beth comes home.

g ....Jack phones the Rescue Team.

h ....Sheila stops the car at Ralph's Stone.

i ....Mia finds Beth's phone.

j ....Sheila and Jack come home.

k ....Mia reads the story of *The Moor Stones*.

l ....Sheila shows *Stories of the Moors* to the girls.

Project work

1 Learn more about the North York Moors. Make a poster about them.

2 Write and draw two more pages for the story (pages 52 and 53).

3 You are Beth or Mia. Write an email to your parents or make a video for your parents.

4 Find all the clocks in the book. Then make a timeline for the story.

The first day
3:00 p.m.
Mia and Beth meet Jack at Baysdale Farm.

↓

8:30 p.m.
Mia says, "Thank you very much!" after dinner.

↓

10:00 p.m.

?

↓

The second day
9:00 a.m.

5 Write new words for pages 50 and 51 in your notebook.

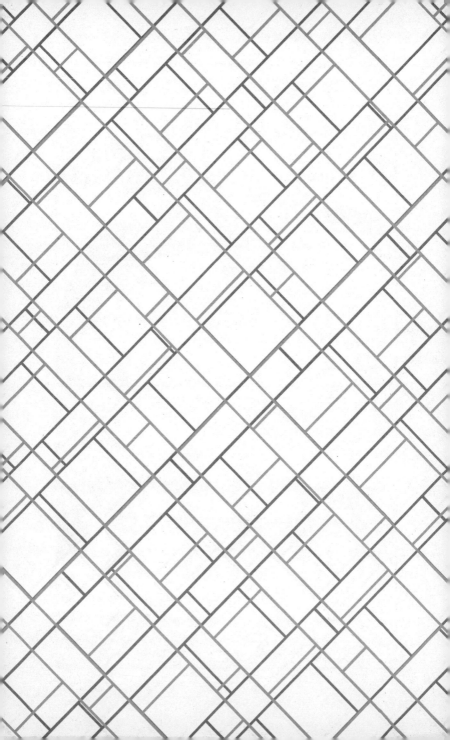

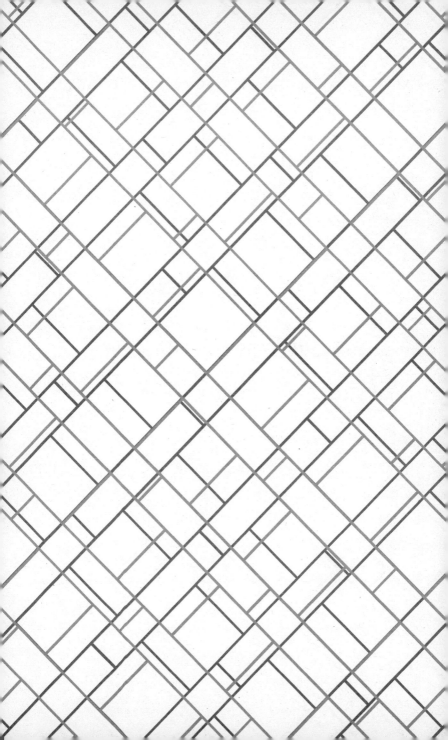

Penguin 🐧 Readers

Visit **www.penguinreaders.co.uk**
for FREE Penguin Readers resources
and digital and audio versions of this book.